To Francis and Vincent

—L. M. S.

For my brother, Jeff, who can fix anything

—M. I.

Henry Holt and Company, LLC
Publishers since 1866
175 Fifth Avenue
New York, New York 10010
www.henryholtchildrensbooks.com

Library of Congress Cataloging-in-Publication Data
Schaefer, Lola M.
Toolbox twins / Lola M. Schaefer; illustrated by Melissa Iwai.—1st ed.
p.   cm.
Summary: Illustrations and rhyming text introduce a variety of tools, and the father and son
who use them to fix everything from a squeaky step to a drawer that sticks.
ISBN-13: 978-0-8050-7733-9 / ISBN-10: 0-8050-7733-2
[1. Tools—Fiction. 2. Repairing—Fiction. 3. Stories in rhyme.] I. Iwai, Melissa, ill. II. Title.
PZ8.3.S289Too 2006   [E]—dc22   2005020254

First Edition—2006 / Designed by Patrick Collins
The artist used acrylic paint on illustration board to create the illustrations for this book.
Printed in China on acid-free paper. ∞

1 3 5 7 9 10 8 6 4 2

TOOLBOX TWINS

Lola M. Schaefer

illustrated by

Melissa Iwai

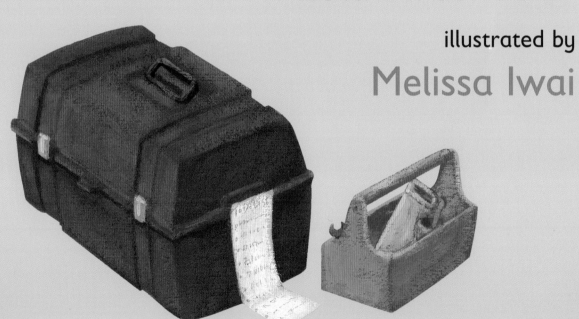

Henry Holt and Company ✦ New York

Dad has a toolbox.
Vincent has one, too.
They are the toolbox twins,
and here's what they do.

With **hammers** and **nails**,
they bang and tap . . .
steps that squeak,
stools that creak.

With **chisels** and **files**,
they shape and scrape . . .

gates that catch,
seats that scratch.

With **grease** and **oil**,
they squirt and spray . . .

wheels that squeal,
blades of steel.

With **levels** and **awls**,
they measure and mark . . .

frames on walls,
shelves in halls.

With **pliers** and **wrenches**,
they turn and tighten . . .
pipes that drip,
bolts that slip.

With **sandpaper blocks**,
they sand and smooth . . .

drawers that stick,
wood too thick.

With **saws** and **shears**,
they prune and snip . . .

limbs that poke,
vines that choke.

With **glue** and **clamps**,
they dab and hold . . .
shoes that flap,
toys that snap.

With **screws** and **nuts**,
they twist and turn . . .

doors that bang,
rods that hang.

Dad has a toolbox.
Vincent has one, too.
They'll use them again . . .

when there's more work to do.